BELLECOUR

CITY SERIES 2

 Canada Council for the Arts **Conseil des Arts du Canada**

ONTARIO ARTS COUNCIL
CONSEIL DES ARTS DE L'ONTARIO

Guernica Editions Inc. acknowledges the support of
The Canada Council for the Arts.
Guernica Editions Inc. acknowledges the support of the Ontario Arts Council.

JOHN CALABRO

BELLECOUR

GUERNICA
TORONTO — BUFFALO — CHICAGO — LANCASTER (U.K.)
2005

Antonio D'Alfonso, editor
Guernica Editions Inc.
P.O. Box 117, Station P, Toronto (ON), Canada M5S 2S6
2250 Military Road, Tonawanda, N.Y. 14150-6000 U.S.A.

Distributors:
University of Toronto Press Distribution,
5201 Dufferin Street, Toronto (ON), Canada M3H 5T8
Gazelle Book Services, White Cross Mills, High Town Lancaster LA1 1XS U.K.
Independent Publishers Group,
814 N. Franklin Street, Chicago, Il. 60610 U.S.A.

Typesetting by Selina.
First edition.
Printed in Canada.

Legal Deposit — First Quarter
National Library of Canada
Library of Congress Catalog Card Number: 2005921431

Library and Archives Canada Cataloguing in Publication
Calabro, John
Bellecour / John Calabro.
(Cities series ; 2)
ISBN 1-55071-216-0
I. Title. II. Series: Cities series (Toronto, Ont.) ; 2.
PS8605.A43B45   2005   C813'.6   C2005-900849-0

FOR SANDRA, LOUIS, CLAUDIA,
AND BASILIQUE SACRÉ–COEUR

ACKNOWLEDGEMENTS

I wish to thank Luciano Iacobelli for encouraging me to explore the art of writing, Antonio D'Alfonso for helping me understand the art of writing, and Sandra Lisi–Calabro for trying to understand this author.

We do not remember days . . .
we remember moments.
Cesare Pavese

I walk. Head hazy. A murky pool of drunken, tripping, half-chewed, disconnected, leftover thoughts. The numb feeling at the back of my head persists and my now scraped-empty stomach aches with the aftermath of convulsing.

Don't stagger as much anymore, swagger from side to side, I avoid hitting lampposts and try to feel better. The darkness is blacker, soothing, befriending me. I need to walk.

The dirty metallic shutters reappear more often, almost on every second store, all of them varying shades of grey. Orienting myself in this black and white neighbourhood is difficult. Shutters, leaking rust, display faded, barely legible names and logos hiding behind peeling paint. The filth and desolation are more prevailing and maybe because of this, I hurt less. The graffiti is bleak, hideous, mostly meaningless scribbles, grey on white, smudges with rounded embossed contours. Illegible. Sometimes, jagged-edged indecipherable lettering; all in all, a poor effort at rebellion. Tossed garbage and broken glass, dark empty remnants of wine bottles, are scattered over an uncaring sidewalk. Imprints of rotting food, squashed by heavy steps, smear the already soiled walkway; footprints acting as pointers. It is an ugly route that I am following.

Torn pages of blemished, dated, yellowed newspaper are flying around, lifted off the ground by a lazy breeze that suddenly comes from nowhere. The garbage circles my elongated, oblique shadow, as it lurches forward, sideways. Half images of truncated moments and thinly sliced words recount, re-describe and re-invent tales of the evening, carving themselves momentary niches through mind-numbing repetition. Words, thoughts and images wrestle for attention, of which I have none to spare.

I don't recognize this part of Queen Street, even the streetlights appear different, older and duller, from another era. My stomach feels fine, no more burning sensations, the defeated acids having been exiled. The storefronts are closed and dark, the only illumination coming from weary lampposts and a reluctant full moon, trying to hide behind slow-moving, thinning, cottons of clouds.

Not all the stores display the shutters of a distrusting neighbourhood on their windows. There is a dark undefended bakery. Inside, shelves mostly empty;

an overlooked baguette on display. A line-up of square tables provides a resting-place for wooden chairs, making it easier for the floors to be swept and washed at the end of a long day.

I pause in front of the window. It doesn't seem possible that patrons might have sat here earlier this evening. It doesn't seem possible that people would even want to live around here. La Boulangerie parisienne has the look of having been closed for a while, and yet at the same time appearing ready to open, and serve hot coffee and chocolate croissants to anxious morning commuters.

These storefronts have French names, which is typical for this part of the city, although there is more French than I recall there ever being on Queen Street, as if the area were trying to redefine itself as the French Quarter, and hadn't told anyone. The side streets also have French names that are vaguely familiar. I try to recall where I have seen them before. The exercise helps me regain some balance and grounds a lingering stoned drunkenness. None of the names prompt any specific memory, just a muted awareness.

I cross a side street and look down. The streetlights are out, perhaps a malfunction. Everyone is asleep, having turned off their houselights, the area is darker than it should be.

My hands don't hurt anymore, and the muffled haze constricting my thoughts is beginning to lift. The swirling images of tonight's hurt are slowly fading giving way to a clearer picture of a present moment. Walking in the dark is good.

There are no trees either, giving this residential neighbourhood added inner-city sadness. No grass, no flowers, just aged, ruptured cement sidewalks. I read the street signs out loud as soon as I can decipher them, my voice keeping me company. I have a feeling that if I call out their names, it will trigger a brighter memory and anchor me to a stronger sense of reality. My weak eyes, made impotent by the darkness of the night, make it more of a challenge than it should be. One side street sounds familiar.

At this distance, I can make out the outline of the first part of the street name *Bell* . . . Perhaps Bellwoods. I know that name. I get closer and decipher the full name: *Bellecour.*

Rue Bellecour.

Rue Bellecour is the name of the street I grew up on in France. The one that crossed my neighbourhood behind Place de la Bastille, west of Montmartre. Bellecour is a common French name and although unusual, it might be found here on Queen Street. Around me there is no one else, there has not been anybody for a while. The streets are deserted, but I am not afraid; there is too much familiarity to this area. I feel that I could know my way around, and that eases my misgivings, and if needed, I still have the gun. I have seen myself here before. I look around and don't recognize anything and yet remember everything. It is rue Bellecour. I am right under the sign. As if knowing that there could be a doubt, against the bricks of the corner building, the traditional French street sign of white lettering on a dark blue oval background reads rue Bellecour. I look north and although it is not as dark as the other ones, barely lit, Bellecour is no less gloomy. It doesn't appear like a typical residential street. The street is neither fully industrial nor commercial or even residential, but a mixture of all three. There are no houses per se, but fronts of buildings with large portals to accommodate the entry of small cars and smaller pedestrian lanes between storefronts. Front yards and porches have gone missing. This neighbourhood is out of place on Queen; you might find it in Europe, maybe, but not here in Canada, and certainly not in Toronto.

I walk up Bellecour.

Rue Bellecour starts with a small corner apartment building modelled after the Parisian seventeenth-century low-rise buildings, those with thin wrought iron wrapped around their windows. It has five floors of cramped apartments, three on each floor from what I can remember. Some face the street and their windows are covered with makeshift drapes, mostly old bed sheets; this is not a rich neighbourhood. The first-floor narrow corridor leads to the back of the building where a small courtyard is overlooked by the other inner apartments, and where on any given day, you can see clean washing of old clothes drying out, limp, hanging from window sills. I know these apartments, have been in them.

Right beside the apartment building, an auto repair shop shows off its mascot. The Michelin Tire Man, perched on the roof watches over the entrance. He is not the new, trim, Michelin Tire Man you see in Toronto today, but the old fat one, made chubby by oversized tires for a stomach that you would find in the Paris of 1963. I feel happy at seeing him again and I put my hand up, a childlike wave, acknowledging the sad familiarity. I have seen these metallic garage doors before; they are old, now rusty, with thick padlocks to keep them shut down at night, but they weren't always like that. Who would want to steal tires, I remember asking myself before I knew about the value of things. There are more Michelin logos and various ads and placards strewn around the out-

side of the building to indicate its corporate associa-
tion, to identify itself as a misplaced bona fide peddler
of high-class tires.

I leave Queen Street behind me, which might be
a mistake. One more won't hurt. As I move further
away from the main street, I forget about the evening.
I don't feel pain anymore. I don't feel anything. My
bandaged wrists, soaked in drying blood, are no longer
bleeding. They don't even sting. My fingertips took the
worst of the abuse; they look ripped-skin awful, but
there is no pain. I walk on, sober at last. Dominique
lives around here, but I doubt I will find her.

I approach the auto repair shop. It has no name,
and I remember it without a name. It's closed. The
wide grey metallic shutters are tightly locked. I used
to run my fingers against them, feeling the grime-
filled grooves as I walked along, transferring, to my
mother's dismay, the dirt from my fingers to my face,
to my clothes. How many times did I walk home this
way, doing this? Surprisingly there is no rust on these
awnings, just dust, covering the still new aluminium
grey peeking out from under the filth. I wipe away
the dirt from the shutters to prove their physicality,
their newness, and my hands blacken instantly, mixing
soil, grime and blood, but I don't care. I wipe it all off
as best I can on my pants, repeating an old memory.

A square dish of light in front of the entrance to the small office is on, like always, lighting our play area. Monday will be business as usual, I am sure. The workers in their blue overalls will expertly change tires, look for leaks by dunking them in a steel vat of cold water. They will look for signs of freed bubbles rising to the surface, betraying an accidental puncture. I liked watching *les ouvriers* search for bubbles.

I see myself there, trying to spot those tiny air balloons before they do, but I am never quite sure. I don't speak to the workers. They know I am here, watching them. I am *le curieux*, or *le petit gamin*. They don't seem to mind having a curious kid watch them. Later they get rid of balding tires, and install shiny black ones, some with a thin white stripe, on old Citroëns and Peugeots. I am not like the other kids; I like to watch, to dawdle placidly, in no hurry to get home. I observe the mechanics at the start of the week with their clean dark blue overalls, their names sewn over the left breast pocket, identifying them as Louie or Paul. I know these men by sight and by their tags; they are friendly and wave as I walk by. The Michelin Man supervises them as they whistle, and joke. They say adult words like *pute* and *tes couilles* and make obscene gestures towards each other.

As a child, I watch it all with a small smile.

I walk on. The street is full of old black and white memories, full of cracked photographs.

Here is another small storefront that I recognize; the barbershop. It has the traditional swirling red and white symbol, announcing its trade. It has no name either, or at least I was too young to know its name. I look inside. The lights above the mirror are left on overnight. There are two prodigious swivel chairs; old black ones made of thick hide. I recognize the long combs, sharp scissors, bottled jells and powders on the small marble ledge of the two sinks. In that wall-to-wall mirror, I can see everything behind me. Sitting on a wooden box, placed on the oversized chair especially for smaller children like me, I feel as if I were at the centre of something, and I almost don't mind sitting still for such an excruciatingly long time.

The adultness of the shop seduces me, and makes my haircuts more enjoyable than they ought to be. Frayed by deep cuts and drooping, there is the black leather strip that the barber used to sharpen his long, switchblade-like curved razors. Shaving tools that both attract and frighten me. The place looks like it has been used recently. On the back wall there are various posters of Le Tour de France. There is a framed black and white picture of the French squad as they pedaled across the Seine and into Paris in

1960, autographed by the captain of the French Team, Roger Rivière. *Le coiffeur* loves to listen to bicycle racing, cheering Rivière on. It is his passion, his escape, and he vicariously travels around France with his team. Cutting my hair, the radio on, he smokes non-stop, a Gitane in his mouth, the open blue pack on the counter, ashes and clippings all over the floor.

I like coming here even when it is not my turn to get a hair cut. He lets me hang around.

"He's no bother," he says to my mother.

I can still smell the brillantine he uses on my hair, as well as on everyone else's. Below the posters, the two chrome, vinyl-covered chairs are side-by-side, waiting to be occupied by customers discussing the previous night's soccer results, or reading *Paris-Match*. Most of the magazines on the side table are photo-romances, tragic love stories dramatized using photographs of popular stars caught in black and white actions and emotions. They are soap operas on paper, whose small, eight-on-a-page pictures and stilted words are followed by millions with anticipation. I am too young to be interested. The *coiffeur* also has magazines for *les petits*; he keeps all my favourite comics. *Rin Tin Tin,* the adventures of a German Shepherd, being the very best.

Beside the barbershop is an entrance to an inner courtyard. On the other side of the entrance is Colette's dressmaker shop and even farther down, at the corner of the street, a dingy little Arab café, with one lonely, and probably still shaky outdoor table. Two wicker-laced chairs waiting for a thirsty Arab or a desperate Frenchman, around it.

It is a small, compact, dark and empty block of familiarity. I walk to the corner, past the two empty chairs, but have no volition to venture outside the *quartier*. There is nothing on the other side. I walk back to the gated courtyard and I accept what my senses have known for quite a while. Almost totally faded, on a blue ceramic background, against the bricks, where it has always been, is the number 18.

18 rue Bellecour.

Of course, I am in front of 18 rue Bellecour. Where else would I be? The iron-gated entrance is locked, but I know that I can put my small hand through the bars and reach inside for the bolt, pull up and sideways until it opens. My hands know exactly what to do. The gate is unlatched but I hesitate, and then, resolute, feet planted, using my bandaged hand, I slowly push. Creaking plaintively as it always had, the door careens to the left, away from me, pivoting on oversized rusty hinges. We childishly relished the crashing sound of metal on brick, and often let that old portal slam against the wall, but not tonight. I stop it from hitting the entranceway, not wanting to announce my presence.

A single light bulb, at the end of its own electrical cord, dangles gently back and forth as it casts shadows along the narrow passageway, below a vaulted ceiling. I remember this entrance as much wider, much taller, not as bleak. Above this gateway, the two-storey building is connected. I hesitate. The breeze continues to play with the hanging light bulb, swinging it back and forth, motioning me, calling me inside, beckoning me to follow it deeper into the courtyard.

I take a few steps forward and feel fine, the world doesn't suddenly come to an end, the ground doesn't open up in front of me as I have imagined it might. I take more small steps, make my way towards the inner rectangle of the courtyard. My feet re-acquaint themselves with greying, uneven cobblestones. The memory of this place knows me as well as I know it. There are wooden stairs on the right that lead to a long, overhanging balcony, and to the upstairs apartments. They go up a dozen steps and then fork to the left, and to the right. I almost expect to see Foxy come forward to greet me, happy, wagging his long thick tail. I wish that I could see him again, pet him. Foxy is a big German Shepherd, almost as tall as me, well almost as tall as a nine-year-old kid.

As I plod towards the centre of the court, I spot a small shadow sitting on the stairs, half way up the first landing. I should be afraid to approach ghosts, but I am not, fears and anxieties having been replaced a while ago by a muted bewilderment. It is not as if I am sure of what I see, or of anything for that matter, but in a quiet way this is as normal as anything I have seen and experienced all night. I am less of a stranger here than I was at Left Bank, the bar on Queen Street, the one I had been at earlier this evening; the bar where Dominique walked out on me, maybe for good; the bar where she asked if I ever got tired of living a life in-between, and for which I had no answer.

Abdullah.

Abdullah, that's him sitting on the stairs. I recognize that shadow, his baggy short pants, and the sleeveless shirt he was always tucking into a crinkled, elasticized waistband. You can't miss knowing that it is him. Abdullah, with his tall wiry body, dark, pocked-marked face, and tight curly black hair, is sitting there; front tooth missing.

"Abdullah," I call.

Ignoring me or maybe not hearing me, he opens his mouth, chortles and then cackles with the laughter of an old man. A peculiarity that does little to ingratiate him to the French kids of the neighbourhood, those in the next-door apartment who hound him mercilessly.

His father owns the Bistro français at the corner, the one with the unstable table. He had been a rich Algerian, a merchant and a barkeeper, who had done well catering to the French colonials. After the revolution, he fled Algiers. The nationalists hated him, having branded him a collaborator, the clerics despised his trade and the French were no longer there to purchase his goods and protect him. Abdullah's father had smuggled out enough francs to start a new life in Paris, but here everything is different. The French do not support him as they had in Algeria. He opened this bistro, and makes enough to feed his family, but it is more difficult than he expected. Respectable Frenchmen do not drink at the Bistro français. His customers are poor immigrants, like my father, who stop on their way home from the local Metal Foundry; a few drunken *clochards*; some pensioned one-drink-stay-all-night regulars and morally weak Muslims, who look both ways before walking in.

Abdullah, his only child, has more money and

more candies than any of us and is expected to share his father's slow-to-be-earned profits with the other kids in the neighbourhood. The French kids pretend to like him at first, and he willingly apportions his goods with them, hoping to create friendship. He is wrong. As a pack, they descend on him, devouring whatever he has to offer, and then turn on him, ridiculing the coarse curls on his head, the smell of curry on his clothes, and his choice of God.

The French kids of our *quartier* are children of the meanest and poorest of the Pied-noirs, the French colonials who, like Abdullah's father, escaped Algeria. They come with nothing, resting in our neighbourhood before moving on, believing themselves better than they are because of nationality and skin colour. These Pied-noirs, a miserable lot, hate everything about the Algeria that had expropriated them. They despise Abdullah and his family as they despise all Algerians. They plug their noses and shake their fists, when Abdullah and I walk by.

The little French bastards hate me too, even though my name is Juliano. Italians are no better than Algerians in this neighbourhood, well maybe one notch above, except for those who befriend Arabs.

"Enculé, enmerdant, nègre, amant des arabes." They volley insults at us.

Abdullah lives in the back of the bistro, his living room and kitchen separated from the bar by a bright curtain over a narrow opening. Everyday, I smell the couscous and the stew that his mother cooks and serves in the bistro. Sometimes I eat with them and that makes me happy.

It is easy to become friends with Abdullah; amiable, he just wants someone to play with, and he has toys, while I have none. When these born bullies, sons of Pied-noirs, find us straying from the courtyard, they circle and push us around, taking our cookies. They flick away our caps and call us "dirty Arabs." It doesn't bother us too much because we have each other.

I don't think that one has a choice as to who to befriend in this neighbourhood. He is the only boy my age in our courtyard, the only other child is Annie, but she isn't allowed to play with Algerians.

Staying within the confines of the courtyard is safe, if limiting. All in all, and for a while, we have a normal childhood.

There I am with him on the stairs, playing with the bottle caps we collect from his father's bistro. We have organized them into colourful Roman legions and prepare them to do battle and to annihilate. In our bottle cap battles the French always lose, it is an indissoluble rule, a testament to our loathing for our tormenters. I have just carved through the pagan, Druid worshiping, disorganized hordes of Gauls, when Abdullah, as the losing general Clovis, takes a break to spit down below, as he often does. The gob hit its target, the doorknob of Annie's "we-don't-like-Algerians" apartment and that's when he starts to laugh. He suppresses his cackling long enough to explain his idea.

"Je sais quoi faire."

We stop playing and move the squatting, multi-spiked, armies of bottle caps aside. He opens the little paper bag containing the round cookies that his father sells for ten *sous* and the hard candies that he grabs from the glass jar. The candies are sold for one *sou*. We lay his goodies on the stairs as if they are fresh troops ready for a better war.

He then makes a great gob of spit and lets it drop on the biggest cookie. The saliva slowly hangs over the unsuspecting treat, suspended in mid-air for a brief moment by a thinning string of spit, until breaking loose it plops dead centre. He laughs, claps, picks up that first soiled cookie and puts it beside the bottle-cap soldiers.

"*Voilà!*"

Abdullah then pushes another sweet under his spew-churning mouth, and lets more slobber fall on target. He asks me to join him, and although I worry about the consequences of fighting back, I unleash my own gob on the innocent *friandise*.

Repeating our actions, we take turns until all the confections are laid side by side on the steps of the upstairs apartments, smeared with venomous spit. We watch our new army of anti-French mercenaries dry in silence, awaiting our command to attack, feeling the gravity and tension of their new mission. Once completely dry, we put the tainted delicacies back and close the small paper bag. We are now ready to share.

They greedily devour our modified goods, never suspecting, while Abdullah and I exchange knowing glances. We follow a pattern of soiling cookies, reluctantly giving them away, laughing, and spoiling others.

Childhood is good.

Coming home from school alone, rounding the corner of Lafayette and Bellecour, I spot them too late and they easily jump me. Before I can run to the courtyard, the four little French Pied-noirs are on top of me, they pin my arms behind my back, and slap my unprotected face with uncharacteristic force. I become a victim of their escalating bullying.

"Stop, stop," I yell. "I'll tell you a secret."

It is a bad idea, born out of self-defence.

"You have nothing to say to us, and we have nothing to say to you."

"No, listen. Jean will want to know."

They pick me up and deliver me to the meanest of the lot, Jean, their leader by virtue of his size. He grabs me and shows off for his gang by slamming me against a parked Renault. He fakes with his right and punches me with his left; to the great amusement of his friends.

"No, wait, it's about you guys. Listen." I desperately scream.

They stop and not even thinking that it is wrong, I tell them about Abdullah and what he's been doing to the cookies, without mentioning my complicity.

"That fucking Arab bastard."

I avoid further abuse from them by betraying Abdullah. They want revenge and I should say no, but it is too late. Jean's plan is simple. After school I am to entice Abdullah to come with me and steal apples from Madame Pigalle's backyard; something that we did regularly anyway. They will lay in wait, jump us both, let me escape, and teach him a lesson that he'll never forget; using the stealing as an excuse. The gang agrees that it is a brilliant strategy, worthy of General de Gaulle.

"Don't you agree, Arab lover?"

"Yes."

"Then you're with us."

No, I hate all of you is what I think, but instead, out of fear, pretending to be one of them, I say, "*Oui.*"

Abdullah, agile and full of energy, quickly climbs the tree and throws down to my waiting hands the best ones; apples that I know we won't get to eat. Apples I needlessly place in a neat pile against thick intertwining tree roots.

"Juliano, this is fun."

"Hurry, hurry up." I say, keeping an eye out for the bullies.

"Ass-fuckers!" The words explode.

"What are you doing here, stealing again, you dirty, ugly, fucking Arabs," Jean shouts, as his army of Pied-noirs rush in.

They tussle with me, but easily, and as agreed, I push my way through them and take off. I don't go far and hide, curious to see what they are going to do. Jean climbs up, snares Abdullah by the neck, and forces him into the waiting arms of his young buddies. It is only at this point that I realize that I was wrong, that I made a mistake, and that I want to take those moments of weakness back.

Luck is on my side. Scrawny and slippery Abdullah, always resourceful, manages to squirm his way out of the mêlée and runs from the horde. Jean is in accelerated pursuit, followed by four nasty baby-Pied-noirs. Abdullah is bolting towards me, dashing for the safety of our courtyard. He is a fast runner, I know they won't catch him, and I am happy to see that he is going to get away from their malice. As if his escape will negate my betrayal.

I should go help him, run interference, but, fearful, I don't. I let my eyes guide him towards me, cheering for him silently. He outdistances them, turns back to see how close they are, while bounding into the street to cross rue Bellecour. Meters from safety, I am ready to befriend him again and to swear never to betray.

Two steps into the paved road, his head fully turned, mocking his pursuers, I watch in stolid horror the slow motion of an inevitable impact, of screaming tires, of a muted thump and of a body in the air, sent there by the front bumper of a grey Citroën.

A black rag doll, all arms and legs, erupts in pain

and takes forever to come down. And when the body of Abdullah finally hits the stone – a weak yelp.

Something cracks and he stops whimpering.

His silenced body bounces once more and crumples a couple of feet away from my side of the curb, a few feet from me; face down, smaller, bloodied, and lifeless.

"Nom de Dieu. Pute. Nom de Dieu."

The driver jumps out of his car, hands in the air, disoriented, looking for help.

"Au secours. Au secours."

Abdullah does not respond and neither do I.

Everyone is running towards the accident. More screams.

The mechanics, Paul and Louie, from the garage, in their dirty blue overalls come out to see what happened. Everyone is in each other's face.

"Merde."

"Call an ambulance."

"Il a mal."

"Hurry up."

They point, they yell at each other, but in confusion and in shock, no one budges. From every corner they rush to take a look. I can't see him anymore.

Attracted by the noise, curiosity at last enticing him to leave his post behind the bar, Abdullah's father slowly makes his way towards the gesticulating crowd. A path opens to let him through, and quickly closes behind him.

I get up from behind the Michelin tires where I have been hiding, to see better, but instead I hear the mayhem-piercing cry of a father's agony.

Damaged and ignored, I leave Abdullah, and go to the courtyard, to my hiding place under the stairs. Time splinters. People's feet are smacking fast and hard, down the wooden stairs pounding above my head as I sit underneath in the dark, slowly giving birth to guilt.

The ambulance's two-tone siren screeches to a halt, waits a solemn moment and starts wailing again. More footsteps, going the other way.

Abdullah dies and I caused his death. It is an accident. People are sorry and give their condolences. Some are even sorry that I have lost my friend, but I say nothing, not a word to any of them, pretending not to understand.

The car that hit him is the one in the little black and white photo that I showed Dominique, the one where Abdullah stands tall beside a sad nine-year-old Juliano.

A photo that I had lost, and found recently.

The driver is from the neighbourhood, a butcher,

whose car was parked in front of Mademoiselle Colette's shop, where we took the picture that summer. They all know him.

"It wasn't your fault," his friends tell him, "Just an accident after all."

The poor man is devastated.

"I didn't see him," he keeps saying, "Darting in-between parked cars, how could I see him, it wasn't my fault."

"Damn kids," the small woman says.

"Un petit voyou," they whisper.

"That Arab boy was always trouble," someone else retorts.

No one questions me, but I know that it is my fault; I've killed Abdullah, and only I know the truth.

My mother, cranky, uncomfortably pregnant, a choir of negativity and cursing the bearing of children as well as the infernal summer heat of 1963, says nothing about the accident, except that it is God's will. Her usual expression for what she cannot, or will not explain. My father shakes his head, and keeps his vow of silence.

Eventually, Abdullah's grieving family moves away and the Pied-noirs, old and young, are happy to see them go.

Tonight, I have nothing to say to Abdullah. What can I tell him? What will sorry mean to him?

He gets up and walks down the stairs and into the back of the Bistro français, into his home, to his mother's heavily-spiced and unpatriotic cooking, safe for the moment.

I walk past the empty stairs.

*

The motorcycle is still in front of Annie's apartment, covered with a black heavy plastic canopy. I don't remember it being uncovered, but always hidden under a dirty and dusty shroud; a depressing monument to a dead son. The wrap is black, but years of dust have changed the colour to a dull-grey. At first glance, Annie's apartment, number two, appears vacant. The window behind the motorcycle is draped in thick, seldom opened, dark-green velvet. It is her parent's mothball-scented bedroom. I go to the smaller window, the one on the other side of the locked front door, the one half-concealed by the stairs, attracted by a sliver of light sifting through. I step carefully around discarded spider-webbed wooden crates meant to carry wine bottles, home delivered on three wheelers once a week. The flickering beam comes from the living room and once closer, I hear the rumblings of the projector. The light shines against the wall, hitting a white sheet used as a screen, receiving the long scratches of the blank portion of a film, the muddled section preceding the start of a movie. The black spots become more pronounced, and quickly overwhelm the sheet. The movie starts. It's a black and white Western. The credits flash instantly and brusquely. They are in English.

The film is an old one, which Annie and I have seen before.

Her older brother, the one standing beside the projector, the one with the brush-cut and mock turtleneck, the pale one, the one that didn't die, is our projectionist. He loves those Hollywood films. He plays them again and again, for himself and for us. He treasures those small canisters filled with dreams, the fantasies of the stoic, neglected son. He can't say anything. How could he even think of adding to his parents' pain by selfishly complaining of being discarded?

They are always American films, some dubbed in French, some silent. The Westerns are his favorites. He has a chest full of them. We watch with him. The same cast of cowboys, Indians, tame horses, stagecoaches, wild horses, chiefs, Apaches, Cheyenne, hard-working ranchers, bad guys dressed in black, good guys dressed in black and sheriffs with shiny badges, recreated the Old West for us. A make-believe world that becomes our sanctuary.

After Abdullah dies, Annie's mother, who is the concierge of our complex, tells my mother that I can play with Annie, and if I want to, watch movies with them. Something about the Arab being out of the way – they mean dead, but no one uses that word. I, like Annie and her brother, love those movies and am grateful for being allowed to watch them. It takes me away from the shadows of Abdullah, from my betrayal, and from my growing guilt. The sadness in the house is also fitting, a home still in mourning because Alain, the oldest son who was slated to become a policeman, had died in a motorcycle accident a year earlier.

I should also be in mourning, but instead, through those movies, I imagine myself as the brave, lone cowboy. Sauntering into town, doing what I have to do, leaving before the town folks could thank me; always a reluctant hero. As the lone cowboy, I speak very little, have a permanent scowl, and ride away into the sunset. I am the quintessential Shane, except that he, unlike me, would not have betrayed Abdullah.

Annie and I are about the same age. She has shoulder-length, soft, wavy hair adorned by an over-sized pink bow that dwarfs her head. She is a small child for her age. Her parents are concerned about her smallness, wondering when she will grow taller; their worries end when Alain dies. After that, her height just doesn't seem important. She wears loose pink dresses without pockets that Mademoiselle Colette makes for her from leftover material. She is not allowed to play with dirty Algerians. Italians are okay. Her parents know my mother because she washes their clothes to earn a few extra francs. Either they like me or feel sorry for me. Her mother imagines that I am good company for poor Annie and take Annie's mind off Alain. Madame speaks of him as if he were still alive, burning daily candles on a makeshift shrine constructed on top of a dresser, lighting sad photographs of an adored first child, Alain's bruised, dust-free helmet to one side. Her parents adopt me to absolve themselves for ignoring Annie. They leave us alone. Annie's brother sits on a chair beside the projector, makes the frequent reel changes and fixes the broken film. No one has a television set in our courtyard, and watching films is a privilege. I am grateful. Annie and Foxy are my only two friends after Abdullah dies, not that I want friends or that they are really friends; more like silent companions.

Annie and I sit on the floor, in the dark, watching Indians perpetually chasing new settlers, the stagecoach, or some poor cowboy venturing into ominously marked sacred land. We wait to see which arrow pierces his heart. She takes hold of my hand, frightened by the sight of murdering Indians scalping a poor settler's family, while the homesteader is away in town buying useless supplies that will not make it home.

Our hand holding starts as a way to assuage her fears. It later becomes a ritual of film watching. She initiates the hand grabbing. I don't mind; I am the brave one, a tough nine-year-old cowboy, already a killer. One day I kiss the back of her hand, just like the gentleman cowboy did on the screen, and delighted, she kisses me on the cheek.

The Indians are on the warpath again.

I go to Annie's to watch Westerns, but like clutching her small hand even more. Hers is the only hand I remember holding at 18 rue Bellecour. Demonstrating affection is not something my family does. Something about my mother's assertion that all touching is sexual and is to be avoided.

I like sitting on the floor, in the dark. It is familiar and warm. Her home is more spacious than my parents' tiny one bedroom apartment. A never-opened closet lets out the smell of the mothballs that Annie's mother spreads everywhere. I feel safe and wanted here. Maybe I take the place of the missing third child, but it doesn't matter. I don't even mind the smell of mothballs. Sitting in the dark, we are witnesses to many massacres.

The Indians howl, burn, kill and pillage with pleasure and abandon, brandishing crude tomahawks, unleashing hundreds of feathered arrows at dust-clouded, blazing-fast stagecoaches.

Close ups of war-painted, menacing, screaming Indians are interspersed with those of frightened bonneted women and cowering pioneer children inside the stagecoach, huddled together. We know there is going to be bloodshed; besides we have seen this movie before.

Annie accidentally brushes her hand against my crotch while trying to find my hand.

The driver and his partner are fighting back uselessly, trying to escape their fate, aiming their powerful Winchester at the terrifying red men. They pick them off one by one, being good Hollywood marksmen.

She finds my hand and holds it like she always does, but only for a short while this time. She lets it go and props her hand between my legs. I don't move. I don't mind. She waits for a moment longer and then takes her hand away.

There are too many Indians riding bareback, circling around the stagecoach; taunting the out-numbered white men.

Her hand comes back, feeling, searching in the dark. She finds an opening along the wide pant leg of my shorts and puts her hand through it. Inside she rests it on my crotch, cupping it from outside my underwear. She probes around, touching blindly, following contours and elevations. Not so much caressing as exploring.

Horses collapse, folding under their front legs; Indians are thrown over their horses' heads. Arrows and bullets are killing at will.

I sit stone-like, fearing that her brother might turn around and see us. I am afraid to lose the privilege of watching movies. She finds the edge of my underwear easy to slip her hand under. Finally she puts her whole hand inside my underpants and begins to fondle my small, uncircumcised penis.

A well-placed arrow kills the driver of the stagecoach. The Indians are getting closer to their prey.

Defenceless white women and children will soon be at their blood-thirsty mercy.

She is very gentle, almost as if she knows what she is doing. She pulls on my foreskin, trying to make me longer. I don't do anything, not moving, limp, afraid to attract attention. I don't really know what I am supposed to do.

The dead driver's partner puts his Winchester into the side holster and grabs the reins of the out of control stagecoach. An Apache manages to jump on board, but a kick in the face sends him flying. Moments later, he is crushed in a close-up of the stagecoach's murderous steel-belted wooden wheels.

I enjoy the warm hand now gripping my small-boy penis. It is no different than holding hands is it?

And when all seems lost, we are shown the dust of a charging cavalry, galloping at breakneck speed to save the women and children from sure death. The music tells us that they will be saved.

I like the feeling. She mostly holds it tightly inside her warm closed hand starring straight ahead.

The cavalry is now chasing the Indians that had been chasing the stagecoach and the movie is quickly over. The black scratches on the wall indicate the sudden end.

She removes her hand.

I come back often to Annie's place, no one pays attention to us. Mostly we watch Westerns, sometimes it is Laurel and Hardy, and other times "Charlot" and his funny cane and hat.

For better viewing, Annie and I sit hidden by the candle-lit shrine of a dresser, with our backs against the wall. We have a different ritual now. Sometimes to make it easier for Annie, I unbutton my fly and she inserts her hand through that opening to find the edge of my *culotte*. She snakes her hand in there until she finds my penis, waiting for her. I let her touch me but I do not touch her back. She knows what she is doing, making it grow longer, and I let her, knowing that it is wrong, done in darkness and in secret, never talked about. She does not look any happier while doing it. Her face is as sad as the house. It is the warmth that I recall and that I like; the gentle touch. I would like to put my hand between her legs and feel her warmth, make her happy, but I am scared.

I go so far as to put my hand between her legs from the outside, on top of her skirt. She does not react and feeling stupid, I quickly remove it. Sometimes she does not want to touch my penis and just holds my hand in the dark, real tight, leaving fingernail marks. I like that as well.

It does not last.

One day, she stops touching me. Later she stops holding my hand. And even later, she stops inviting me to see movies in the dark with her. Her parents greet me, friendly, but do not call me in. Annie has told her mother that she does not want to play with me anymore, that she is getting too old to watch idiotic movies with silly little boys. She would rather play with the older boys and girls, the Pied-noirs in the next apartment building, even if they are mean to her.

I don't think that I did anything wrong. Yet I accept the consequences. I was there at their pleasure, and am ostracized at their whim. Perhaps in some ways, I am being punished for what I have done to Abdullah. They realize that I am a bad person, and I really can't blame them.

My parents are no help. Busy complaining about the heat and a due date that never comes, my mother doesn't question or even notice that I stop playing with Annie. My taciturn father keeps his words in check. He does venture one day that the new owner of the Bistro français has raised the price for a glass of wine, and that it isn't fair.

The flickering light of the projector stops. Annie's brother turns the projector off. The movie is over; they are finished for the night. The lights inside Annie's apartment go out.

I walk away from the window and turn to my right, towards the steps leading to the upstairs apartments, numbers five, six and seven are up there. I look under the stairs where I hid from people when I was younger. The cavity is small and filthy, but I know that I once found comfort there, a place to hide anger, grow guilt and fight childhood desperation. I try to understand how I became so bad.

Unhappy, lonely, I retreat into the make-believe world of my comic books, pretending to be Lancelot or some other valiant knight, misunderstood but wanting to be courageous. Thinking that given another chance, I might become braver.

Gingerly, tentatively, feeling heavy with the malaise of many years ago, I climb the stairs. The old wooden steps are still creaking. I am afraid someone will hear me, and look furtively around, but everything is quiet; no one is here. Remnants of the dark-blue paint, like burst scabs, are peeling off the banister, exposing the black veneer underneath it. I try to scrape some of the paint, but it doesn't peel off like when I was younger. The steps are smaller than I remember them, not as wide or as high. There is a small landing where the stairs fork to the left and to the right.

The four or five steps to my left lead to apartment five, to that tiny, one-and-a-half room apartment my parents called home in 1963.

Apartment 5 is the smallest in the complex, not much more than an oversized closet. A diminutive kitchen occupies a corner of the entranceway to the bedroom, where my mother has squeezed a small table with two chairs. From the table, if I stretch, I can touch the chipped, enameled two-burner stove-top attached to a portable gas tank, crammed beside a sink we use for both dishwashing and face washing. The rest of the apartment is the one bedroom where we all sleep.

I don't want to go there. I don't want to see myself standing on the other side of a closed front door, screaming and crying for a missing mother. She has gone to the open-air market for fruits and vegetables, and has left me home alone for what she thinks will be only a few minutes. Those few minutes of abandonment become a distorted moment that lasts forever. I scream and cry for her to come and get me, to pick me up, but she isn't there and can't hear me.

The neighbours come out, and hearing the pain of an infant, try to console me from the other side of the door. Nothing works. No one has the keys. I continue to wail. It isn't my mother's fault, she doesn't know better; a poor village girl, out of place in a foreign city. I sob, keeping a vigil at a door that will not open. The voices on the other side only serve to alarm me and heighten my fears that she has lost her way, that she has gone forever. Exhausted, I crumple behind the door. When she comes home, she tries to explain, but I do not forgive her. I choose instead not to love her, never to cry again.

I remember my bed against the length of the room, the side closest to the window, the wall that looks into the balcony of the courtyard. A plastic sheet hangs on a clothesline to separate my section of the room from my parents' bed. There is a space the size of the door between our two beds that lets you in the room. I hide in that plastic cocoon and read the exploits of Obélix and Astérix. In my cot, I dream of being a Roman soldier, never the emperor or the commander mind you, always the Roman soldier, the one with the crested helmet, the one who obeys orders. Sometimes I wish we were rich, like my father had promised. I wish that someone would buy me a Roman helmet for Christmas or for my birthday. Celebrating birthdays, like hugging, is not something that we do, and no matter how much I selfishly pray for those toys, they never come. Where is God when I need him? I stop praying and quit listening to my Thursday morning Catechism classes. I lose myself in the many adventures of *Rin Tin Tin, Olivier,* and the medieval outlaw, Thierry La Fronde. I read anything that the barber lets me take out of the shop. I am grateful for the *coiffeur.* A kind man, he tries to give me a lifeline to escape the darkness of 18 rue Bellecour.

Towards number five is not where I want to go. I decide to go the other way, turn right and walk up the steps towards apartment six. I also know this apartment quite well, the one with the blue door; an elderly woman named LouLou lives there, all alone, all in black. She seldom comes out. People deliver whatever she needs to her front door. Opening it barely a crack, just enough to squeeze in the brown-bagged groceries, she looks out in fear before quickly closing the door. The kids say that she is a witch, but I don't believe them; she is just old and scared. I have no significant memory of her and, tonight, she does not appear.

★

The front door to apartment seven has a small round window, too high for me to see through as a nine-year-old child. Now taller, I see a yellow glow in the hallway lighting the entrance to the bedrooms at the back of the apartment. The larger window looks into the kitchen. The lacy, white curtains are drawn closed, but I recognize the silhouettes inside. Monsieur Robert is there with his wife. They are sitting at the kitchen table, talking in low conspiratorial voices. He is wearing his favourite slightly frayed cardigan and dark-brown corduroy pants that are two sizes too big. He looks as if he has lost weight. Monsieur Robert laughs and whispers to his wife. His thinning grey hair is combed straight back, held down by a good dose of *brillantine.* Madame Robert's hair is tied back in a chignon; an apron dangles from her neck. A low hanging light bulb centered in a wide-brimmed pink metallic dish hovers over the kitchen table. I spot the bright-red open box. They are bending over an elaborate construction set called Mecano, totally absorbed, hiding a partial structure. It could be anything. One can never be quite sure with Mecano, you add to it and it changes in appearance. Not unlike memories. As she leans back, Madame reveals the Eiffel Tower, one-third completed. It is our project; she has no right to be working on it.

It is unusual to see Madame Robert there. She is never home when Monsieur Robert invites me to play with his Mecano set. He says she is out "*au marché*," or visiting her elderly mother "*dans la banlieue*," far away, but there is Madame Robert adding a link to our Eiffel Tower. I think that Mecano is our hobby, he says that it is for us men, not for women. He has made it sound like we were special. He is a great teacher, but I always suspect him of lying.

I have problems with the small bolts and screws that hold the small, elongated metallic pieces together. My fingertips are sensitive, but my fine motor control skills have been slow to develop. Monsieur Robert is very patient, helping me to do it right.

He takes my little fingers in his long hands and helps me twist the screws on. He shows me how to keep in place the bolt, with one finger and how to gently rest the nut on the tip of another finger. He teaches me to wind the nut onto the immobile screw, with a half turn of the finger holding the nut. Once engaged, I release it and twist it as tight as possible with two fingers. It is tricky for a young boy. When I get better, we build bridges and tall cranes. The crane has a working pulley with ropes. This is more complicated. Once done, we take the structures apart and put all the pieces back in their right place in the large box with separate compartments. Monsieur Robert is fastidious, and proud of it. I love that Mecano set. I am hoping that, one day, he'll give it to me as a gift.

The one drawback is that while playing with the construction set, I have to listen to his stories. He tells me stories about WWII and stories about his wife. He tells me how he was almost caught by the Germans. The stories are all different but they always end up with him getting away from *les Boches*, in the nick of time. The one story he is particularly fond of is the one where he was a French Resistance Fighter traveling though a forest, going from Grenoble to St. Étienne. He got off the main path to relieve himself. As he was squatting between the trees, hidden from the road, he saw *les Boches* walk right where he had been, not a moment before. That *pute de merde* saved his life, he said. He had a new attitude towards bodily functions from that day on.

He also has a vitriolic dislike for the Italian army and its inability to put up a decent fight. I never fully listen or understand the stories. I am too busy joining the pieces together, making sure that they do not fall. If he notices any inattentiveness on my part, he stops, shakes his head, looks at me disappointingly, and asks me to sing *La Marseillaise*. I have no choice and, quite out of tune, sing:

> *Allons enfants de la Patrie*
> *Le jour de gloire est arrivé.*
> *Contre nous, de la tyrannie,*
> *L'étandard sanglant est levé,*
> *L'étandard sanglant est levé,*
> *Entendez-vous, dans nos campagnes,*
> *Mugir ces féroces soldats*
> *Ils viennent jusque dans vos bras*
> *Égorger vos fils, vos compagnes.*

And at that point he joins me for a rousing: "*Aux armes citoyens!*" Louder:

> *Formez vos bataillons,*
> *Marchons, marchons!*
> *Qu'un sang impur*
> *Abreuve nos sillons.*

Satisfied, he laughs and allows me to continue playing.

Most days, I sit alone on the balcony across from his window, my legs dangling over the edge, reading or looking down. Annie's apartment is directly below. She isn't there. Abdullah is dead. Lonely, with no friends except for Foxy, I watch the courtyard.

Monsieur Robert sees me from his open kitchen window and invites me to join him:

"*Juliano, viens, viens.*"

I go.

"*Aujourd'hui nous allons faire la tour Eiffel,*" he says, all excited, having bought additional Mecano parts.

"Juliano, did you know that we would need eighteen thousand pieces and two and a half million nuts and bolts . . ."

He sounds like a very important professor.

"To equal the number of rivets and steel pieces used on the real Eiffel Tower, I mean, if we wanted to be accurate?"

"*Non, Monsieur, je ne savais pas.*"

He tries to impress me with his knowledge, and he does. We begin our new project. I don't mind his war accounts but don't understand the other stories, the ones about his wife, which are just as strange and unbelievable.

Methodically, we build the base. At some point he stops talking about architecture or engineering and watches me. I can feel his eyes staring. I try very hard to join the parts the way he has taught me to do it, and hazard ignoring him. He gets an embarrassed look on his face and, at that point, I know he is going to start talking about his wife.

"Yesterday, do you know what I did, Juliano?" he asks, expecting an answer.

Always the same start. I know what he has done, but pretend not to. I never get enough of playing with the Mecano set. I don't want to go home and hang my legs over the balcony, wishing I had friends. I want to finish the Eiffel Tower. It is important.

I say, "*Quoi, Monsieur Robert?*"

Without looking up from the tiny bolt that I am tightening with the special key that comes with the Mecano set, I give him the answer that he wants and it makes him happy to think that I am interested.

"Madame had to go to the washroom, but I wouldn't let her, I stopped her," he laughs an ugly belly laugh.

As a kid I don't laugh much, and adult laughter shocks me, puts me ill at ease. This is not even funny.

My head is down, I don't want to look at him when he gets this way.

He says, "Juliano, are you listening?"

"*Oui, Monsieur.*"

"I kept detaining her, at first I asked her to get me my slippers. I had hidden them and it took her quite a while to find them. She had to find them, she is my wife, her duty; you know that, right? When Madame had almost given up, I told her that I thought that I had seen them in the closet. I only said that when she was the furthest away from the closet, so that it would take her even longer to get them. I am not stupid you know."

I put one more link to the second level platform, and am ready to leave, "*Je dois rentrer, Monsieur. Je m'en vais.*" I am on my way out, pretending that I want to be home.

"*Reste.*"

He won't hear of it, getting exasperated, continuing his monologue.

"Madame was getting really annoyed and kept telling me that she had to go pee badly. I got angry with her, saying that if she knew where she put things I wouldn't have to suffer, that I could not find my things and that it was all her fault, that she made my life miserable. I raised my voice."

What is he talking about?

"Juliano, I started an argument with her, she could not leave in the middle of an argument. Poor woman, she felt so bad. She sat on the corner of the chair, crossing her legs, you see, Juliano, just like this. She begged me. Let me go or I am going to burst, she kept saying, I am going to pee myself, and I pretended not to hear her."

He is so proud of the way he tells his story. There are no bathrooms in the apartments; we all share the same bathroom at the end of the balcony, an austere old one with just a hole and two cement steps to set your feet; a lanky faucet in the corner to wash your hands. She would have had to go outside, I know that.

"I yelled at her, told her how she made me miserable, that one day I was going to leave her. She crossed and uncrossed her legs and started swaying. I knew she was ready."

He interrupts himself and says, "Juliano, are you listening?"

I am not sure.

"*Oui, Monsieur.*"

"When she finally got up to run to the bathroom, I ran after her in the hall and caught her just before she opened the door."

He pauses, takes my hand and insists that I go see the very spot where he caught her. It is always a couple of steps away from the front door, in the hallway. Once there he lets go of my hand, which I am thankful for. He has unattractive long, bony fingers. Breathlessly, red-cheeked, he continues.

"Listen, Juliano, I grabbed her right here, I squeezed my body against hers, I could feel her tensing up, and I said to her: 'Don't worry, *mon petit chou,*

54

it's okay, relax, if you go outside now you will not make it to the washroom, you will pee yourself before you reach the bathroom. It will be embarrassing. Do it here. I will go get the chamber pot. Just relax. I took too long, on purpose, Juliano. I saw it in her face. She was peeing and looked upset. I said, I am your husband, it's okay. She was ashamed, but I kept saying that it was okay. I reassured her. She hid her face in my shoulders while she peed. Her body relaxed and I put my hand under her skirt, under her underwear, and felt the warm pee running down my hand. Juliano have you ever touched pee as it comes out of a woman. It is so warm and nice; I just let it run over my hand until she stopped. Are you listening?"

"*Oui, Monsieur.*"

It is important to him that I listen. If I am to be called again to play with the Mecano set and finish *la tour*, I have to lie and continue to be a bad boy, a good listener.

"Some people don't like the smell, but not me, they say it smells bad, not me, some people in Africa drink it. Did you know that, Juliano? I don't mind touching it, but drinking it, that's another story. I put both my hands inside her underwear. They were all wet, Juliano. Have you ever touched a woman's wet underwear? You should, it feels so good," he says with feverishly misplaced glee.

He moves his head up and down and tells me in hushed tones.

"I don't have to tell you, that I had a huge boner, but, Juliano, this is between you and me. It's between us men, you can't tell anyone. It's like the Mecano set, it's for us men, it's between you and me. You should try it sometimes, there is nothing like it. Maybe you can start with your own pee. Well, it does not matter . . ."

He looks blankly into the distance.

"I am tired, Juliano, you go home now."

I quickly walk out. I don't like seeing him that way and I am glad to be near the door.

That night he died.

My mother tells Mademoiselle Colette that he dropped dead of a heart attack, "Suddenly, massive."

"In the kitchen," Annie's mother says, "No warning and he wasn't that old."

"It was the cancer that I had been worried about and then this."

Madame Robert sobs, unable to control her tears.

I don't know a thing about heart attacks or cancers; in the confusion no one explains, but there is a funeral and we all attend. The neighbourhood is crying; he was well liked. But I don't cry. I don't feel anything except surprise that a lot of people are dressed in black, smelling of mothballs, just like Annie's apartment. More importantly, I am upset at having to leave the tower unfinished.

I don't think about what he said; I'm only nine. Monsieur Robert was harmless, predictable and overzealous in his patriotism. I can't even say that he told true stories. All his tales ended with his wife peeing, and him somehow having orchestrated the drama, touching her wet panties.

I went along with it. I should have stopped going to his apartment, but I didn't fully understand. I did wonder if it was selfishness that made me a bad person? Was wanting to finish the Eiffel Tower a really bad thing? I loved that construction toy. He had hinted that he would give it to me, but died before he could.

Instead, Madame Robert gives me an orange when she sees me after the funeral. Oranges are nice, but what I really want is that Mecano set.

I stare in the window again as if looking for answers; they have turned off the lights. They're gone. It's dark inside. I move away and sit on the landing like I used to sit as a child, put my head on my knees and close my eyes.

★

At the bottom of the stairs on my left is the backdoor to Mademoiselle Colette's dressmaking shop. Like the barbershop and the bistro, it opens onto the main street. I don't remember its name, but she lived in the back where she had one large bedroom, a living room and a small kitchen. The apartments downstairs are bigger than those on the second floor. She is lucky.

A light is turned on. The bedroom window opens into the courtyard and I look through it. She is sitting at her sewing machine, exactly the way I remember her.

Mademoiselle Colette never married. I never see a man in her shop or apartment. She does not need men, she has a beautiful wild beast of a German Shepherd, Foxy, who protects her and gives her all the love she needs – so she tells her neighbours.

Mademoiselle Colette is my mother's age and they became good friends. Mademoiselle Colette teaches my mother a few French words and how to sew. I don't know what Mademoiselle gets in return. I don't think Mademoiselle is well liked in our court-yard. Too gregarious, too jolly, too fleshy, she smokes Gauloise, and lives alone.

"There are no good men left," she complains to my mother. The men she knew had too many faults. Freeloaders most of them, they wanted her meager wealth, unwilling to give anything in return.

Sitting side by side with my very pregnant mother, while I play with Foxy, Mademoiselle Colette confesses that she is lonely, that life is tough, and that she puts up a brave front for the nosy neighbourhood gossips. Sometimes my mother sends me to the dress-shop, and tells Mademoiselle to stay behind. Women come in and ask her about the newest styles from London or Milan, or about the difference in textures, about laces and hats. They flip through fashion magazines. Strident, frivolous but nonetheless passionate, they argue about the merits of modern synthetic nylons.

Mademoiselle takes measurements and hums to herself a Piaf tune; she particularly likes "*La Goualante du pauvre Jean.*" Always under her breath, never too loudly.

Arriving for their fittings, all sizes of women walk around in thick pointy bras and plain white-cotton underwear. They ignore me, or if noticing, throw me the odd "*Qu'il est mignon.*"

Mademoiselle pins their dresses and makes adjustments, while I tease Foxy, my own Rin Tin Tin, my last friend.

It is the summer of 1963. It is very hot in Paris, an uncomfortable scorching forty degrees by day and not any better by night. A white-hot heat they call *la canicule*, a temperature they haven't seen in fifty years. Mademoiselle makes plans to go to her house *en campagne*, to cool off. The second week in July, as for most of the French, is the beginning of her annual vacation, but this year Mademoiselle Colette stays in the city.

"Not this summer," she says with a lit Gauloise hanging out of the corner of her very red mouth, "Too many orders to fill before Bastille Day. Too many outfits to make."

Ashes dangle, threaten to drop, but miraculously stay put.

She bemoans, "Why is everyone getting married this summer?"

Endearingly she blows smoke in my face.

"*C'est impossible.* I can't go this year."

She complains that her vacation is ruined and takes a long drag of her cigarette, freeing the ashes from their tenuous perch, allowing them to fall on the floor. My pregnant mother helps Mademoiselle with the dresses.

Maman is near full term and ready to give birth, earning a few francs washing for Annie's mother and sewing for Mademoiselle Colette.

Mademoiselle tells my mother that I can stay with her overnight when and if she ever goes into labour. I will be well looked after, she says. She could also use the company; sometimes it gets lonely in her large empty apartment. My mother does not mind, easily irritated, vaguely angry with her lot in life, she is glad to have a friend who understands.

My father does not care, and keeps his thoughts to himself. An elective mute, he speaks very little. Early in the morning, this tower of silence goes to work on an old bicycle, comes home late, exhausted, a quick glass of red wine at the bistro, two more at home, and soon after he falls asleep. Maybe he suspects that I killed Abdullah, or Monsieur Robert, or at the very least that I am bad luck. He wants nothing to do with me. As usual, he leaves trivial child-rearing decisions to my mother.

It is quickly arranged, early in the morning, before she leaves in a taxi for the Hôtel de Dieu, near Sacré Coeur, where Parisian women go to give birth, I will spend the next few nights with Mademoiselle.

I like eating at Mademoiselle Colette's. The food tastes good, very different from what we have at home. There my throat seizes up on tripe soup; I gag on the fatty pieces of meat my mother throws in the stew. Eating what we can afford. We have pasta; most days topped with bitter broad beans, dandelion leaves, or large chunks of blemished potatoes and soft onions. At Mademoiselle's, it is different. She cuts out the fat for me and does not care if I do not finish my meal. Buys fresh bread from the *boulangerie* across the street, unlike my mother who has learned about day-old baked goods at half the price. We have artichokes and aspara-gus with mustard sauce. Later, she serves plain yoghurt, soft cheese and a *petit gateau*. Mademoiselle likes over-sized portions served on oversized plates.

At suppertime, my mother is still in the hospital.

I sit across from Mademoiselle and watch her put green beans flaked with parsley in her mouth; she makes eating appear wonderful, exciting. A few drops of olive oil dressing squirt out of the corner of her mouth and she daintily wipes them away. She talks to me as if I am an adult, says that the merchants she buys from are trying to rob her blind because she is a woman, increasing their prices with each new order. They blame post-war inflation and immigrants, and she damns them. Mademoiselle Colette chews with enthusiasm; her lips twisting, contorting and dancing around mouthfuls of chocolate mousse cake.

"And lace, we won't even talk about it," she says, shaking her head.

"My customers don't want to pay, they ask for credit. What am I made of . . . gold? And that Madame Pigalle, she is the worst. When am I going to see any money from her? I have to compete with the new stores, they import the dresses, they don't make them in the shop like I do, they're from a factory. How can I compete, Juliano? I work hard to make an honest franc."

I listen to a mixture of complaints, self-affirmations and simple philosophies, while she uncorks another bottle of wine.

She says, "*Tu comprends, mon petit Juliano, la vie est dure . . .*"

"*Oui, Mademoiselle Colette.*" But I don't understand much. Still, I like watching her, being with her.

"Madame Pigalle wants to look twenty years younger, and she thinks that a dress will help her. She is wrong, she is old and should accept that. Do you understand these women, Juliano? I can't work miracles. I can't do much when a woman weighs over one hundred kilos, can I, Juliano?"

I laugh at the thought of Madame Pigalle stuffed into a dress at least two sizes too small.

"You understand, Juliano."

I say, "*Oui, Mademoiselle.*" Happy to please her.

She carves herself a slice of Camembert and pours another glass of Beaujolais.

"Without wine there is no life."

We toast.

"*À ta santé, mon petit.* It's good for the heart."

She looks at me watching her.

"*Tu es un beau garçon, Juliano, tu donneras du plaisir aux demoiselles.*" She winks.

I keep my head down and eat. She drains her wine, ends her gulps with a satisfied smacking of the lips. The button on her shirt has popped open and she hasn't noticed. I can see parts of her white bra and get a small peek at her large breasts. I don't say anything. I peep there once in a while.

"*Pardon,*" she says, as she gets up and walks away, using the back of the chair to steady herself.

When she comes back from the bathroom she has buttoned up her blouse and smeared on more of that very red lipstick. Refreshed and with new vermilion lips, she disdainfully shoves the dishes in the sink. I help her clean up the table.

"*Tu es si gentil.*"

She pats my head and I like the feeling of being helpful, of being good.

Her bedroom smells of baby powder. Foxy saunters from room to room, looking like a big bad wolf and I imagine him so. I, the brave hunter-warrior with his companion wolf. I put the back of my head against his growling furry belly, and read the new *Obélix*. I listen, with Mademoiselle's permission, to the Tour de France on the large Marconi radio. Tired, I lie on the bed between the big frilly doll and the small pillow that she puts there for decoration, and close my eyes. Her bed is so big, maybe big enough for five people, I think. I don't take up much space. I am a small kid. I spread my arms and legs, make angel wings, enjoy the expanse of the bed.

The night does not bring relief from the heat. The Marconi says that France is having a record heat wave, and Paris is not spared its share of casualties, mostly old people, shut-ins, are dying by the dozen. Drink plenty of water, listeners are reminded.

"*Mais on va mourir, putaine de canicule.*" Mademoiselle swears as she walks around, cursing the heat, unbuttoning her blouse. She drinks wine, says that it is better than water, and that this bottle of Beaujolais is particularly good.

The fan perched on the dresser does not help, and

placing it on a chair, she brings it closer to the bed. Later, she mixes up an old family recipe of cold water with large chunks of lemons and hard bread. Sweetens it with spoonfuls of sugar and brings it to me. We drink from the bowls. The lemons make us pucker up and we laugh about it. She takes care of me in a way that I am not used to.

Before bed, she removes the doll and pillow from the centre of the bed and turns the cover over. She pushes it to the foot of the bed, leaving the sheet. I take off my clothes and put them on the chair beside the bed, like she tells me to do, and lie down in my underwear.

"I'll come to bed a bit later. *Bonne nuit, mon petit.*" She kisses me on the forehead.

Tossing and turning, I finally fall asleep under the watchful eyes of Foxy, who keeps guard.

Her snoring wakes me up. Curious, I sit up and look at her. Mademoiselle's shoulder-length hair is down, disheveled. She has light skin, rosy cheeks, and a long white negligée, all basking in a bluish moonlight. She is on her side, her back to me, her face towards the door. I see her thick shoulder, her massive back, and wide naked legs. She had thrown off the sheet during the night. The negligée bunched up around her waist uncovers with the help of the fan, her large thighs. *Mon Dieu*, she is big. The moon shines through her nightclothes exposing naked buttocks. I didn't know people take their underwear off at night. I try not to move, not to wake her. Mademoiselle Colette stirs and pulls her legs up against her stomach. Her back to me, the moonbeams find a path between her legs, lighting a dark patch of hair between her large bottom cheeks. I didn't know there is hair down there, or that there is a purple-pink wedge of flesh trying to peek from a bush of black hair. I feel as if I am doing something wrong looking at that part of her body. I try to look away, but my eyes keep going back there. I can't avoid being bad.

I close my eyes, not wanting her to find me looking. I stay still without taking a breath, trying to get sleepy. With my eyes closed I turn towards the wall and away from her. A moment later, restless, I turn around again. Open my eyes and I am looking right into her face. Surprised to see a close-up of her naked face, from which she has removed her rouge. I examine her pencil-thin eyebrows and her dull crimson lips. Her face looks puffier. I notice the outline of her large breasts under the negligée. The outside light goes right through the material. I discover a raised nipple in a circle of darker skin, centered on a flabby breast. Her left breast is fully uncovered, displaying tiny little bumps and a few black hairs around the nipple. I look down at her large stomach and underneath it. There, I find the source of the hair I had seen earlier. She has a lot more hair between her legs; a bush of dark, curly hair. Ashamed, I look away.

An empty bottle of wine and a half-full wine glass are on her night table. She twists, turns, snorts and stops snoring. I can't fall asleep; kept awake by the heat, by her body so close, by the strangeness of sharing Mademoiselle's bed, by fear. Her eyes are closed and I smell the pink dust she dabs on her face and on the rest of her body before bed. The heat is as intense as ever. I look at her plump body, soft, welcoming, scented with baby powder, glistening. She turns her back to me. Attracted to her, I inch closer to a mountain of flesh, thinly veiled by a see-through nightgown. Will she wake if I get any closer? If I touch her? I turn my back to her so that I can pretend an accidental touch. We are now against each other, back to back, cheek to cheek, tiny me and large Mademoiselle; a slight veneer of wetness, of sweat, forming where we touch. She does not wake; I hear her heavy breathing. I stay that way for a while but I'm not satisfied. Roused, braver, I turn around. Her deep breathing encourages me to continue my exploration of her body. I push myself against her, curl up behind her, spoon-like, and find a womb of warmth, a cosiness I have not experienced before. Satisfied, welded to her, I fall asleep.

She turns around, wakes and gently pushes my warm body back to my side of the bed, while I keep my eyes closed, pretending to be asleep.

I wait for the snoring to start again, open my eyes and look. She's on her back, her white negligée wide open. I can clearly see the wild mane over-running the whole crotch area, more hair than I could ever have conceived of. Her breasts, flattened, are cascading on each side of her chest. I sit up to better peek. Mademoiselle's mount of a belly lies imperially above a valley-full of hair between fat thighs. Fascinated, unabashed, I stare at her enormous, sleeping body. What would it feel like to be on top? I extend my hand towards her large squashed-down breast. I listen to her breathing, look at her closed eyes. Quickly touch her nipple and withdraw my hand. I shouldn't do that, but her breasts look so soft, asking me to lightly caress them.

I am afraid that Mademoiselle Colette will wake up, but the fear is not enough to stop me, if anything, it agitates me. Suddenly she moves and I quickly turn around. She twists to my side and we are both facing the window. My head is just below her breasts, I can almost touch them if I move up a bit. Surely it would be an accident if our bodies brushed against each other. It isn't enough. I roll back and face her. Open, close, and promptly re-open my eyes. Mademoiselle's nakedness is in full side view. I pretend to sleep, but I move my leg towards hers. Nothing happens for a long while. Dormant and unaware she moves her leg, and it touches mine. The feeling is warm and clammy. Hot wet naked skin against hot naked skin. I crawl closer. My whole body, in full length is attached to her sweaty flesh. I don't mind the feel of sweat and I don't care if she sees me. My head to the side of her breast, her nipple fastened to my cheek. My small penis is against her hairy clump, ensconced against a furnace of flesh, her heavy breathing above my head. We are one body. Can she not sense me as I feel her? I try to match my breathing with hers, but keep losing the rhythm. I move down. My hair brushes her ample, round belly. My legs touch the lower parts of her meaty thighs. I am trembling.

Annie said that a man should lie on top of a woman because it gives the woman the greatest pleasure.

I lie still for quite a while, pondering what Annie

had meant, and then gathering my nerve, I move back up to put my cheek to hers. As I maneuver up and rub myself against her body, thinking of Annie and her hands, my penis gets harder and longer. I like that. My closed lips are now pressed against her breasts. Impassioned, I lightly suck on a waiting nipple, as if wanting to draw milk, while at the same time enjoying the sensation of a stiffening penis. I try to push harder, but Mademoiselle stirs, detaches herself from me, turns away, and lies on her stomach. Perceiving that she doesn't want me, coming down, I return to my corner and fall asleep.

I wake to the gentle shaking of the mattress. I look to the side with sleep-veiled, half-open eyes. Mademoiselle Colette has grabbed the small, decorative pillow and has placed it between her legs, hiding her pink folds, hiding her black short curls. Her thighs are wrapped tightly around it. She moves it up and down, between her legs, making the bed squeak.

Her breathing is different than before. It is louder, more pronounced, uneven; her belly begins to shake. One hand is to her breast, grazing a nipple; the one I had kissed. She has it between her fingers and is pulling; gently caressing her chest. Unsure as to what she is doing, excited, another erection beginning, I move nearer. Her eyes are closed. My body is now again along her side and moves up and down with the bed as she grinds the pillow against her twisting body. She must know that I am right there beside her. I touch her to let her know. Mademoiselle grabs me, plops me on top of her, and removes my underwear, all in one swoop. She discards the pillow and uses me instead. I keep my eyes shut and let her rub herself against me. I am getting harder and harder and it feels good. She uses her legs and her thighs to cosset me against her crotch, and holds my body in a vice against her. My head is flattened against her breast. Smothered, gasping for air, I find it hard to breathe. She lets me go and I am able to turn my head to the side. She tries to position me so that her hairy tuft grinds against my penis. She lifts me up, grabs my penis. I let her, passive, pretending to sleep. I feel good; it can't be bad. Mademoiselle tries to position my penis along her inner thigh, using her fingers, trying to guide it inside of her. She stops and makes an upward thrust while holding my penis with one hand, tight against her. It goes inside an opening between her legs but as she jerks to the side, it comes out. She tries again, getting the same results. My penis keeps coming out, longer, but nine-year old small, it is too wet. Inflamed, frustrated, her breathing gets shorter, and faster. Holding on tight, she is pushing me up and down, inside of her, outside of her. Jerking up and down, all eager, I lose control and let go, releasing a first-time ejaculation all over Mademoiselle Colette's belly.

Mortified, I try not to move, not to breathe. I lie very silent, on top, as if to deny I was involved. Gently, caringly, she deposits me to my side of the bed and does not say anything. I open my eyes to see. Hers are still closed. Mademoiselle stays on her back, spreads her legs wide apart and puts her large hand where I had just been. At first it is quite gentle, then it becomes faster and faster, two fat fingers going in and out. At times she slows down, lingers inside by twisting them, and then she starts a rapid open-palm stroking. Her whole quivering body is now again going up and down in one motion, following the rhythm of her fingers. She gropes wildly at her breast, at her mouth. Both hands are working in unison, working her into a frenzy. She goes faster and faster until she lets out a scream, opens her eyes and suddenly stops, sees me looking at her. Grins, stops twitching, and squeezes tightly both hands between those weighty thighs, her eyes and smile still on me. I try to get close to her body, but she turns around and rolls away. After a while, I hear her snore.

At breakfast we have a bowl of café au lait. She

puts *confiture* on my toast, and passes it to me. She is happy. It is strawberry jam, my favourite. Everything is fine. Mademoiselle does not say anything about the night before and neither do I, and as we finish our *petit déjeuner,* she looks up and says, "Juliano, I almost forgot, I saw your father while you were sleeping, you have a brand new baby sister. We will have to go and see her."

She buys me candies, comic books, and feeds me gourmet meals as if nothing happened, but at night she relegates me to a small foldout cot that she places against the wall, far from her bed.

My mother comes home, no less irritable, although her belly is a more manageable size. She now spends her days neglecting me and nursing the baby.

It wasn't just Mademoiselle's mountain of sexual comfort, her heavyweight sensuality, the unfinished Eiffel Tower, Monsieur Robert's heart attack, or Abdullah's untimely death that confused me, but also my parents' behaviour. Detecting perhaps that I had become bad, unretrievable, they stopped complaining about my silence, my disappearances, my withdrawal, and simply ignored me. I wanted them to tell me that bad things and good things were part of life, that change was inevitable, that I might be salvageable, that I was indeed a good boy. Instead, they abandoned me to myself, took care of a colicky baby girl and stopped loving me.

Sitting for a moment on the main stairway, trying to make sense of my past, the barrel of the gun digs into my groin, reminding me of the present. I think of Dominique and again wonder who this gun is for – her or me? I take it out, place it besides me on the landing, and close my eyes.

★

It is September and the summer is over; the heat wave is not.

I am standing in front of the ornate, black iron grilles that lead into Le Jardin des Invalides. Two majestic golden lion-heads flank the cobbled entrance. The wide-open gates reveal an imposing sculpture of Liberty dedicated to dead heroes of the French Revolution, colourless flowers, shades of grey at her feet.

School at L'École Frederic Fays started a week earlier but I have no interest in it. Abdullah should be sitting at the small desk beside me. No one speaks of the accident, almost as if it didn't happen. The French kids who had delighted in tormenting us, now leave me alone. Ironically, having no enemies simply solidifies my loneliness, underscores the idea that there is something wrong with me, that the summer has damaged me.

At recess, I can see the girls on the other side of the fence. Annie is there, talking to her classmates, her back to me. On rare occasions, I join the boys and play a variation of cops and robbers, or Indians and cowboys, all moronic chasing games for which I have no patience. I drop out, feigning tiredness, beginning to live in earnest my half-life. Even Jean, still the toughest boy in the group, seems young, childish. I am no longer afraid of him. Over the summer I have changed, become indifferent to childhood and to living. I accept my time alone, and that is why I go to the park by myself.

Contemplating going in, I see him across the street. An older man, looking at me. A well-dressed gentleman with bulging, clean-shaven pink cheeks. We make eye contact and he trots over. He has glasses, small round lenses within a thin metallic frame hooked onto a bulbous nose. Wearing a dark-blue pin-striped suit, a black tie hanging professionally from a white collar, he looks like a typical chubby businessman. He might be any Frenchman.

"*Pardon, jeune homme.*"

His thick eyebrows come closer as he bends down and politely asks me for directions to a small apartment building on rue Jean Jaures. I know the street, it's a few blocks away, and without hesitation, I agree to lead him.

"*Oui, je vous le montre, c'est pas loin.*"

"On the other side?" By that he means across the bridge, on the left side of the river Seine.

"*Oui, monsieur, c'est là.*"

He asks my name: "*Comment tu t'appelles?*"

I tell him, "Juliano."

He has a low gravely voice, and softly clears his throat after every few words. He wants to know my teacher's name.

"Mademoiselle Dubois."

"Oh, I know her, she is a nice teacher. Don't you think?"

To please him, I agree.

More questions follow, asked in such a way that giving answers is the right thing to do, the only thing to do. He is a gentle, kind, engaging, portly old man.

He asks about my favourite subject and I say math. I hear something about nationalities, "*Tu n'es pas français. Es-tu arabe, italien?*"

I thought that it would be wrong not to be French so I lie again and I say very proudly, "*Non, Monsieur, je suis français, je suis né ici a Paris. Ma mère est française.*"

I am confused about what I should say or not say, about when to lie and when not to lie. We continue down the Avenue, turn right on rue Jean Jaures, until we stand in front of an old decaying building. Posters of President de Gaulle, running for re-election, are plastered on the bulletin board of a round sidewalk kiosk, to the left of the entrance.

"Do you know who that man is?"

"Of course, Monsieur, *c'est Charles Joseph de Gaulle.*" Everyone knows that.

"Very good. A great man, you know," he says, while I point to the building he had been asking about.

Happy to show him that I can do something right, that I had not lied about knowing the address. That I can be a good boy. I beam.

"Do you live far?"

"*Non.*"

It wouldn't take me too long to get home, maybe ten minutes, if I walked fast.

"If you have time, you understand, would you come in with me to help me read the names on the doors? Only if you want, you understand? You see my eyes are quite weak. Silly me, I broke my glasses and these, as you can see, are quite old, for distance only. I can barely see anything in front of me. Everything is a blur, that's why I ask your help. I am quite lost without my reading glasses. And you are such a smart boy and very kind. I won't forget to tell Mademoiselle Dubois that you were very helpful."

He says it all rather quickly, looking me in the eyes, clearing his throat with irritating regularity.

I don't answer but follow him inside. He doesn't insist. I go along because he asks me and I want to show him that I am a big boy, and that I can do things right. I am good at reading. That is one truth; I read all the time. Everyone knows that.

We walk up the stairs, an easy climb for me. I am aware that I am still wearing my grey school smock. It makes me look like a sissy little boy. He has a harder time climbing and is already panting, having to rest at each landing. On every floor, he makes a big production of looking for the name of his friend on walls in need of paint. I slowly read the name for him, and inevitably, half way through, he says, "*Non.*" He adds, "*Merde. Pardon, mon petit,*" to show his frustration. An overly polite, insecure grown up child, but the climb is killing him and he tells me so.

We repeat our search on each dirty floor.

The last landing has only one apartment. I am sure that this has to be the person we are looking for. Instead of asking me to read the name on the door, as he had done earlier, he says:

"Let's rest, I am quite out of breath. This damned, *pardon*, heat is going to kill me. *La canicule*, you know."

I sit down beside him on the last stair, feeling sorry for this fat gentleman, sweat pouring down his red face. I begin to feel anxious at being somewhere I have never been. It is not that I do not want to be here; just that it is a bit too unfamiliar, a bit scary. It is also getting late. His thick eyebrows are now drenched in sweat. He wipes his brow with a dainty monogrammed handkerchief and I smell the heat and the sweat on him. He tells me that it is not good for his heart to do all this climbing, his doctor had advised him against it, he says that he might have a heart attack.

Thinking of Monsieur Robert, not wanting to go to another funeral mass, I wait for him to catch his breath, impatient to check the name on that last door so that I can be on my way.

"I have to lie down on my back, for my heart, you

know, otherwise it will stop ticking. Do you mind? I'll just be a minute."

He lies with his short legs hanging over the stairs. On his back he looks like a half-pig, half overturned turtle, a bit monstrous, quite comical, but I don't dare laugh.

He turns his head, looks at me and says sweetly:

"You should try it too, it will be good for your heart. And I won't be the only one looking funny. If you understand what I mean."

I do, and being on my back feels strangely good.

I lie down on that landing with my feet also dangling over the first steps, checking my scraped, scrawny knees, thinking about what to say to make him hurry. Thinking that I have done what I am told, and that for once I am being a good boy who isn't complaining.

And like that, we lie there for a while.

Surprisingly, abruptly, and with a sudden urgency, he sits up and keels over, flopping awkwardly on top of me. There must be something wrong.

Pinned, I don't move. I'm petrified, not knowing, unsure as to what is happening. Is he dying? He's hurting me. Crushed, I am unable to breathe. He must have lost his balance and will soon get off. My nose is against the flab of his underbelly. His untucked shirt exposes salty wet skin, and it makes me gag. I feel sick. He doesn't move. Afraid, I tap his shoulder to wake him and he responds by squirming roughly, unpleasantly. I am suffocating, but he crushes and doesn't care. I can't speak.

Is this what happens to bad boys? I wasn't really a good boy, was I?

As if he knows that I will die if he doesn't get up, the fat man uses his short arms to lift himself above me, allowing me to breathe once again. His fat face, dripping gobs of sweat, is right above mine and makes it almost worse. His blank, frightening face, no longer kind, doesn't see me. Queasy, ready to throw up, I turn to the side but I won't cry. He can't make me cry. I close my eyes instead. He can't sustain himself for very long and his now repulsive body comes crushing down, his clammy weight squashing me again.

I cringe, grit my teeth, and hold down the vile stomach acids that are churning up. He rubs furiously; poking, fondling, touching where he shouldn't be.

I keep my eyes tightly shut knowing that this is how it must be to wait for death, not hoping anymore, wanting it to be over, wanting to meet Abdullah again. Maybe that's how things are meant to be. God's will, my mother would say. Where is she? Where is my father? I know I won't be missed. If I die, maybe people will know that they should have been kind to me. If Foxy was here, he would eat this man alive. He's not here and I want to die.

The fat man lifts himself up yet stays on all fours, my small body between his knees. He waits, thinks about it, and having decided, he pounces. Possessed, brutally, he turns me over so that my face is scrunched against the dirty floor of the landing where it smells like dirt, rotting wood, and . . . like vomit. Unable to hold it in any longer, my insides disgorge violently, hiccuping bile.

There is no pity in him. With renewed and demonic energy he bends and thrusts savagely, impaling me to a bloodied, century old, wooden floor . . .

From below, a door creaks and prevents me from dying.

He detaches himself. The weight is gone. I turn around and open my eyes to see the fat man's face change from excited madness to cowardly fear. Glistening with new sweat, waving a double chin, trembling, he stands over me. The door below groans again louder. About to say something, he changes his mind and pulls his pants up. He holds them with one hand, and quickly bounds down the stairs he had so labouriously climbed up moments earlier.

The front portal opens and then slams shut.

The apartment door on the landing below that had squeaked open, closes abruptly, returning the building to stillness. I don't allow myself to cry, to break this welcomed silence. I don't want to make any noise. Ghostly pale, I sit up very quietly on the landing, resting my chin on two small fists.

Outside the entrance to the building, I am waiting for him. I watch the fat man of my childhood trying to get away from little Juliano, rushing towards me. I position my adult frame right in front of him. Take the gun out of my belt, brought with me for another purpose, and without hesitation I pull the trigger. I aim for his head and shoot him. I shoot the face, the stomach, the groin, and empty the revolver. There are no bullets left. Still I keep firing, pulling that trigger as many times as I can, as quickly as I can. Unaffected, unaware of my existence, the fat man keeps running, and hobbles down the street. He disappears in the dark, running towards Le Pont de la République.

Little Juliano comes out.

Jules, why did you go with him? I ask. You could have run, you were smaller, faster, he was fat and slow.

You could have screamed, there were people in the building, they would have heard you. You could have kicked, scratched, but you didn't. He never threatened you, never gripped your hand. You agreed to go in with him, to lie down beside him. No one forced you. What was wrong with you? You were, and always have been, a bad boy. Admit it, I yell at him.

"Nothing happened. I didn't cry."

The clouds hide the moonlight and I find myself in total obscurity, the blackness of the Paris sky being my only light. Every apartment at 18 rue Bellecour is now completely dark. The only spot of brightness comes from the one light bulb in the narrow walkway calling me out. It is time to leave. I get up from the old splintering, blue blotched, wooden steps, put the gun under my shirt, and begin a slow walk towards the entrance gate; turning my back to the courtyard. My footsteps hit the ground with an exaggerated slap. I want everyone here to know that I am leaving and won't come back.

On the sidewalk, the breeze tries to dry my tears as I sniffle like a nine-year-old child, trying to stifle a torrent of old-new tears. I wipe away what I can, with my dirty, bandaged hands while I hear the gate swing shut behind me, banging noisily against the latch, closing for good.

I lumber my way back to Queen Street and Bellwoods, back to Toronto, walking without words, without thoughts. It is only a block away, but it seems farther. Numb, jaws locked together, I turn left on Queen and walk towards where I remember having parked the car, far away from rue Bellecour. The back of my neck is sore. Thirsty, legs barely supporting me, stiff, stumbling; I find it difficult to move forward.

I walk miles to find my parked car. The faint sounds of music, no longer relevant, are coming from Left Bank, the bar where I had been drinking last night. I get in the car and drive slowly.

I feel the sting of healing cuts and watch a pair of bloodied hands caked with filth steering me away. My face in the rear view mirror is a fright of dirty streaks. My hair is matted and sticking out. I have the look of a madman.

Driving along Queen Street West, the storefronts, without those imprisoning metallic shutters, are now brighter and recognizable. The streets are not as dark as they were earlier. There is more colour, no longer a black and white world. Less graffiti and less garbage on the ground. Morning will be here soon.

The car stereo is playing the same Etta James CD

I began this journey with, and she howls out my favourite, "*This Bitter Earth*." The familiar music restores some normality. I turn the sound way up and scream along, or at least sing the words that at this moment appeal to me. "This bitter earth," I scream.

Faces of my night join together to circle a dull pain. They are all there, in their different sizes, shapes and colours, in their lives and in their hurt. Their distinct faces twirl around faster and faster, intertwining, melting into each other, blurring into one swoosh of streaking shapes and colours. Faces become a merry-go-round of dizzying images. Moments cross time and reality, defying understanding. My legs shake uncontrollably and I pull to the side. My mouth is dry.